XANDER'S PANDA PARTY

by LINDA SUE PARK | *Illustrated by* MATT PHELAN

Houghton Mifflin Harcourt
Boston   New York

Originally published in hardcover in the United States by Clarion Books,
an imprint of Houghton Mifflin Harcourt Publishing Company, 2013.

For information about permission to reproduce selections from this book,
write to trade.permissions@hmhco.com or to Permissions,
Houghton Mifflin Harcourt Publishing Company,
3 Park Avenue, 19th Floor, New York, New York 10016.

www.hmhco.com

The illustrations were executed in ink and watercolor.
The text was set in 19-point Fifteen 36.

The Library of Congress has cataloged the hardcover edition as follows:
Park, Linda Sue.
Xander's panda party/by Linda Sue Park; illustrated by Matt Phelan.
pages cm
Summary: Xander's plan to host a panda party falls through, since he is the only panda at the zoo, but when he
extends the invitation to all of the bears, complications ensue. Includes author's note on the animal kingdom and
the international effort to save pandas from extinction.
[1. Stories in rhyme. 2. Pandas—Fiction. 3. Zoo animals—Fiction. 4. Parties—Fiction.]
I. Phelan, Matt, illustrator. II. Title.
PZ8.3.P1637Xan 2013
[E]—dc23
2012029662
ISBN: 978-0-547-55865-3 hardcover
ISBN: 978-1-328-74058-8 paperback

Manufactured in China
SCP 10 9 8 7 6 5 4 3 2 1
4500671556

To Stephanie,
because Sean loves pandas and she loves Sean

—L.S.P.

For Anna and Maeve

—M.P.

Xander planned a panda party. Yes, a dandy whoop-de-do!

But Xander was the only panda. Just one panda at the zoo.

Xander sat and chewed bamboo. He changed his plans and point of view.

Xander planned a bear affair and thought of all the bears he knew.

"Black Bear,

Brown Bear.

Both the Polars.

Grizzly is a rock-and-roller!

Koala is a little dozy, likes her tree
all leafy-cozy. I will ask her anyway.
Surely she will want to play!"

Xander's party preparations took great pains and perspiration.

Menu

Berries

Honey

Fish

Grubs

Eucalyptus leaves

Bamboo

"The menu needs some taste sensations, plus the proper vegetation!"

Xander handed out the cards:

Calling all bears:
A celebration invitation~
Food and fun and conversation!

From her tree, Koala hollered, "Xander, I am not a bear."
Xander didn't understand her. "Koala Bear, you're not a
bear?" He stared at her in consternation.

"Sorry for the complication. I know I'm called Koala Bear,
but I am not a bear, I swear. I am a marsupial. Marsupials—
we're rather rare. Will I not be welcome there?"

Xander fetched some more bamboo. He wasn't sure what he should do. He chewed a slew of new bamboo; he nibbled, gnawed, and thought things through.

And he planned a hearty party!

"Fur or hair or hide can come. All the mammals, every one!"

Calling all mammals:
A celebration invitation~
Food and fun and recreation!

Soon Rhinoceros sent word:

Xander felt a little blue. He chewed bamboo, a stalk or two. He fidgeted and paced the floor, then scratched an itch and paced some more.

Finally, a firm decision: Xander's brand-new party vision!
"All the birds and all the mammals, from whooping cranes to hybrid camels—anyone with fur or feathers, congregating all together!"

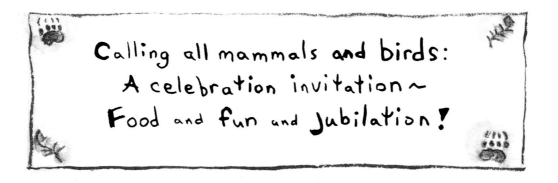

Calling all mammals and birds:
A celebration invitation~
Food and fun and Jubilation!

"Xander," said the crocodile, with a most beguiling smile. "There's a party, so I've heard. You've invited all the birds. Birds and reptiles—long ago, we were related, don't you know? If you didn't, now you do. Can't the reptiles join in, too?"

Xander didn't chew bamboo. Instead, he swithered in a stew.

What to do? His worries grew. Was his party falling through?

Then came a voice from down below, somewhere near his little toe:
"Why don't you ask everyone? I can help you. We'll have fun. Nice
to meet you, Xander Panda. I'm Amanda Salamander."

Amanda Salamander lent a hand to Xander Panda. Xander's party plans went from grand to even grander!

Almost time to start the party—then Amanda squeaked
out, "Wait! What's that coming through the gate?"
A truck . . . a ramp . . . a wooden crate?

Xander didn't have a clue. He shook his head and wondered, "Who—?"

"Hello. Hello. And how are you? Zhu Zi here. Please call me Zhu."

"I'm Amanda."

"My name's Xander. Did you say your name is Zoo?"

"No, not Zoo. My name is Zhu. Like saying 'zoo' mixed up with 'shoe.' In Chinese *zhu zi* means 'bamboo.'"

And Xander knew just what to do.

What a party! What a ball! Lots of new friends,
tall and small! Every creature at the zoo!

Which means, of course . . .

. . . the humans, too!

When my son was eight years old, he became very interested in pandas. He amassed a collection of dozens of stuffed pandas, had panda posters on the walls of his room, and did a research paper on pandas. Together we learned a lot about pandas! I love going to the websites of the National Zoo in Washington, D.C., and the San Diego Zoo to watch videos of their pandas. Both these sites also offer streaming live video on their "panda cam" links.

The taxonomic classification of pandas was debated in the scientific community for many years. Because pandas share traits with raccoons, they were first classified in the raccoon family (Procyonidae). In recent years, scientists have used DNA and molecular analysis to discover that pandas in fact are more closely related to bears, and they are now considered members of the bear family (Ursidae).

Pandas are native to China. The Chinese government has several panda research centers, which protect the animals, study them, and help them breed. China lends some of these pandas to zoos around the world. They are always loaned out in pairs, one male and one female, because it is hoped that the pair will breed in their new home.

Only a few decades ago, pandas were dangerously close to extinction. Captive breeding programs and the combined efforts of scientists in China, the United States, and other countries are slowly increasing the number of pandas; there are now estimated to be about a thousand pandas in the wild, and more than two hundred in captivity.

Pandas have become a beloved symbol of the international effort to save species from extinction.

Bears and koalas are both members of the class of animals known as mammals. The animal kingdom is divided into two main groups: vertebrates and invertebrates. The vertebrates (animals with backbones) are further divided into classes: mammals, birds, reptiles, amphibians, and fish. Each class is divided still further. Within the mammal class, koalas are a type of marsupial (pouched mammal). Other marsupials are kangaroos and opossums.

The oxpecker (*Buphagus africanus*) is a bird native to sub-Saharan Africa. It perches on large mammals, including rhinoceroses, and eats ticks, larvae, and other parasites. The relationship appears to be symbiotic, meaning that it is advantageous to both creatures—the oxpecker gets its meals, and the rhinoceros has fewer parasites—although some research indicates that the oxpecker might itself be parasitic, conferring little benefit on the mammal. In any case, the two creatures are often seen together in their native habitat.

Most evolutionary biologists believe that some of the reptiles commonly known as dinosaurs evolved into birds during the Mesozoic era. Today's reptiles and birds share common ancestors that lived more than one hundred million years ago. The evolution of life on our planet continues to be a complex and wondrous mystery.